MW01049134

THE MAGIC POT

Three African Tales

Retold by Dinah M. Mbanze

With illustrations by Niki Daly

Published by Kwela Books
28 Wale Street, Cape Town 8001;
P.O. Box 6525, Roggebaai 8012

Edited by Jo Bleeker
Cover and design concept by The Inkman
Set in Bodoni 16 on 20
Printed and bound by NBD
Drukkery Street, Goodwood, Western Cape

First edition, first printing 1999

ISBN 0-7957-0099-7

INDEX

THE MAGIC POT

Long ago there was a poor man and his wife. They were so poor that their torn clothes looked like straws. They lived from fishing and hunting, and by digging roots in the veld.

Sometimes they had no food for weeks at a time. So they drank water when they were hungry.

One day the man went hunting in the forest. He was very weak because he had not eaten for days. He knew he had to find food for them, otherwise they would die from hunger.

As he walked in the forest, he came across a big pot. He was frightened by the pot. So he did not touch it. He just stood looking at the pot for a long time.

Suddenly the pot began to talk to him. “Take me to your home,” the pot said to him.

The man was afraid to touch the pot. He was afraid to take it to his house.

"Take me to your home," the pot repeated. This time the man was also afraid to leave the pot behind, so he carried it to his house.

Soon after he had arrived at his home with the pot, it began to talk.

"Mother, Mother, please wash me!" the pot said to the man's wife.

The wife washed the pot until the pot was shining.

"Mother, Mother, please rub me with fat!" the pot said to the wife.

The wife rubbed the pot with fat, on the inside as well as on the outside.

The pot gave the man and his wife many tasks to carry out. They did everything the magic pot asked them to do, because they were afraid of a pot that could talk.

The poor man and his wife had neighbours who were very rich. The poor man and woman could always smell the bread the neighbour's wife was baking. They became so hungry that they had to fasten their belts tightly. With their pinched waists they did not feel the hunger so much.

Then one day the pot disappeared and went to the rich neighbour's house. The neighbour's wife thought it was her own pot. So she put her dough into the pot. She wanted to put the pot on the fire and bake the bread. But when she looked again, the pot had disappeared.

Meanwhile, in the hut of the poor couple, the wife heard a voice:

"Mother, Mother, put me on the fire!" It was the pot speaking to her.

She put the pot on the fire. Soon there was a lovely baked loaf of bread in the pot. She and her husband ate the bread and washed the pot.

Sadly, the poor man and his wife often quarreled. When things got really heated, the wife would take a sjambok and beat her husband until he cried.

One day the poor man was again hunting in the forest. Ee! There was the pot, right in front of him!

"Tell the boys to jump out of the pot," the pot said to the man.

"Boys, jump out of the pot!" the man said. Two boys jumped out of the pot, each holding a sjambok.

They began to beat the man until he cried. When they had done with beating him, the boys jumped back into the pot. "Take me home now," the pot said to the man.

The man took the pot to his house. His wife thought he had brought food, but there was no food in the pot. She became angry and began to shout at her husband. "Boys, jump out of the pot!" the husband cried.

The two boys jumped out of the pot. They chased the wife around the house, beating her with their sjamboks until she cried.

After a while the husband shouted, "Boys, jump into the pot!"

The boys jumped back into the pot.

From that day the woman always spoke nicely to her husband.

One day the rich neighbour sold his herd of oxen for a lot of money. He needed a safe place to hide the money. When he saw the pot, he thought that nobody would look for money inside a pot. So he hid all the money in the pot. After a few days he saw that the pot had disappeared. The rich man looked all over the place, but he could not find the pot, or his money.

The pot had gone back to the poor man's house again! But the poor man and his wife were now terrified of the pot, and of the two boys who each had a sjambok.

The pot spoke to the man. "Open me! Open me!" the pot said.

The wife ran away. The man was too afraid to run. So he opened the pot and found the money!

Now the poor man and his wife began to live like rich people. They ate good food and forgot that they had once been poor. The man began to drink beer and often became drunk.

At the same time the pot appeared in the home of the rich neighbour. His wife saw the pot first and cried, "There's the pot that took my bread!"

The man grabbed the pot and shouted, "This is the pot that took my money!"

He was so angry that he began to beat the pot. Immediately, both the rich man and his wife were pulled inside the pot.

Then the pot ran out of the house and into the deep forest where it threw the rich people out.

When the pot came back to the poor man's home, he saw that the poor man was drunk.

The pot became very, very angry.

"Boys, jump out of the pot!" it said. The two boys, wielding sjamboks, jumped out. They beat the drunken man until he fell down.

"You wasted the money! You are a bad man!" they scolded. "Did you forget the terrible suffering when you had no food for weeks?"

Then the two boys jumped back into the pot and the pot disappeared forever.

The poor man and his wife were poor again.

THE MBULUMAKHAZA

Once upon a time there was a princess who was betrothed to a king. The king lived far, far away.

When it came time to marry, the princess's mother prepared her for the wedding and the long journey ahead.

"You must not talk to strangers along the way. Remember to keep quiet and all will be well," the mother said. Then she instructed a young girl to accompany the princess, so that she, and not the princess, could do all the talking.

The princess was given a cow on which to ride.

Her mother also gave her a branch from a tree and said, "My child, take this branch with you. If you see the branch fade, you will know that I am not well. If you see the branch dry out, you must know that I am dead."

Then her mother wished her well and sadly waved goodbye.

On the first day of the journey, the leaves on the branch remained green and strong. On the second day, the leaves began to fade.

The princess became alarmed.

At nightfall of the second day, the leaves dried out. The princess began to cry because she knew that her mother had died. She stopped the cow and dismounted.

"Moo! Moo! Moo!" bellowed the cow – as though it was crying its heart out.

Below, in an underground hole, was an animal that looked just like a human being. It was a Mbulumakhaza who lived from drinking the milk of a cow.

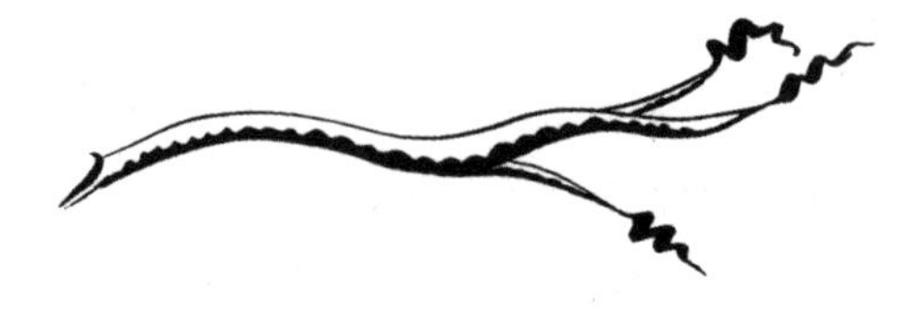

“I hear thunder,” the Mbulumakhaza said to herself. “Let me take a look to see if the rain is coming. I must get some wood to make a fire.”

But it was the cow’s bellowing she had heard. She became very happy when she saw the cow. “If I had the cow,” she thought, “I would have a lot of milk to drink.”

The Mbulumakhaza climbed out of the hole and saw the beautiful young princess and her attendant.

"Ah," she said to the princess, "you look too beautiful! What is this lovely thing you wear around your neck?"

"These are beads," replied the princess, forgetting that her mother had told her not to talk to strangers.

The Mbulumakhaza said to her, "Let me go with you for a short distance. I will turn back at the thorn tree ahead." Then she asked, "May I please wear your beads until we reach the thorn tree?"

The princess handed her beads to the Mbulumakhaza.

The Mbulumakhaza then asked the princess, "What is that beautiful dress you are wearing?"

"This is a wedding dress worn by a princess," the princess replied, again forgetting her mother's words.

"May I try it on, please?" the Mbulumakhaza asked. "I will return it when we reach the first anthill just beyond the thorn tree."

The princess handed her wedding dress to the Mbulumakhaza. It made her very happy.

Then the Mbulumakhaza asked the princess, "What is this beautiful thing on your head?"

"It is a beaded veil worn by a bride to be," she explained and gave it to the Mbulumakhaza.

"May I please ride on your cow?" the Mbulumakhaza asked. "I will give her back to you before the last anthill on the ridge up ahead."

The princess handed her cow to the Mbulumakhaza and they continued on their way. Soon they reached the last anthill on the ridge. Below, they could see the king's palace.

"Please give me back my clothes!" begged the princess.

"I will give it to you when we reach that gate," replied the Mbulumakhaza, pointing to the gate at the king's palace.

The princess became alarmed when the Mbulumakhaza did not return her clothes. She began to sing, "*Mbul-makhazane, Mbul-makhazane, return my clothes!*"

"Keep quiet!" snapped the Mbulumakhaza.

"*Mbul-makhazane, Mbul-makhazane, return my clothes!*" the princess sang.

"Keep quiet!" shouted the irritated Mbulumakhaza.

Frightened by the Mbulumakhaza, the princess walked silently beside her attendant.

When the king saw the Mbulumakhaza, he thought she was the princess, because she was dressed like a bride. He greeted her and invited her into the palace.

The Mbulumakhaza was taken to the king's grandmother who immediately gave her the work of chasing away the birds in the cornfields.

Every time the Mbulumakhaza chased away the birds, she cried, "Shwa! Shwa! Shwa! Go and tell my parents at home that I, Mbulumakhaza, the great drinker of milk, am going to marry the king!"

Days passed, weeks passed, months passed. Then there was some trouble at the palace.

The milk in the pots began to vanish. Then the milkpots vanished! The king's grandmother told her daughters to watch the princess – who really was the Mbulumakhaza, the great drinker of milk. So they watched and caught her drinking all the milk – but they still did not know that she was really the Mbulumakhaza.

The king also told his soldiers to watch the princess – who really was the Mbulumakhaza.

The soldiers hid themselves in the cornfields and listened. They heard the Mbulumakhaza shouting at the birds, "Shwa! Shwa! Shwa! Go and tell my parents that I, Mbulumakhaza, the great drinker of milk, am going to marry the king!"

Quickly the solders reported what they had heard. The king ordered the soldiers to dig a deep ditch and fill the ditch with milk.

Then he called all the women of the palace and ordered them to jump over the ditch.

Only the Mbulumakhaza refused to jump over the ditch. "I have a cramp in my stomach!" she cried.

"Jump over the ditch!" the king ordered. The women all jumped over the ditch.

"Jump!" the king ordered the Mbulumakhaza. The Mbulumakhaza had no choice. So she jumped. But she could not jump over the ditch.

Instead, she jumped right into the ditch and began to drink the milk!

All the women then saw that she had an umsila – a tail – hidden under her clothes.

"It's the Mbulumakhaza!" they all cried.

Immediately the king ordered his soldiers to kill the Mbulumakhaza.

The attendant then dressed the real princess in the wedding dress and the beads and the beaded veil and then she presented the princess to the king.

The king married the real princess and all the people in the palace were very happy!

THE END OF THE WORLD

Long, long ago there was a grandmother who liked to think about many things. One day she stood outside her home and looked at the sun.

Every day she saw the sun come out on one side of the world, and go down the other side of the world. She began to wonder if it was the same sun she saw every day.

The sun began to trouble her.

"If it is the same sun," she said to herself, "the poor sun must be very tired because it works so hard."

But then she thought again: "If it is not the same sun, it must sleep somewhere at night."

The grandmother pondered: "If it is the same sun, the world must end somewhere, and begin somewhere, for the sun has to return every day."

There was only one way to find out. So the grandmother decided to walk to the end of the world and see for herself. She went into her home and packed some clothing and food.

Now she was ready to go and find the end of the world.

The grandmother thought about the direction in which she should walk.

The easiest way was to follow the sun. So she set out, following the sun until the evening.

When it became dark, she looked for a place to sleep. The next morning she got up, ate some food, and began to walk again.

She kept on walking and walking.

Every day the grandmother walked and walked. In the evenings she slept. At night she sometimes dreamt that she was still walking. She became very, very tired of walking, and of dreaming of walking.

Then one morning she woke up, but there was no sun to follow. So she sat and rested.

That night while she slept, she again dreamt she was walking.

But as she had not walked that day, she was not sure if she was dreaming of walking, or really walking. It was most confusing!

When she woke up, the sun was still not to be seen. The grandmother then discovered heavy clouds had come between her and the sun. That was why she could not see the sun!

She was happy walking now, because the sun had not really left her. When she grew tired of walking, she rested.

The next day the sun remained hidden behind heavy rain clouds.

It rained and it rained and it rained.

"I can just as well walk on," said the grandmother, "by this time I know which way to walk."

She stood up, took her clothes and food, and walked on without the sun.

Soon she came to a river. There was a tortoise and a mouse sitting on the bank.

"Tortoise," she asked, "please tell me which way to go?"

The tortoise looked this way, then that way, this way, that way. He pointed to his right. "That way!" he said.

But the grandmother was not sure. "Mouse," she asked, "please tell me which way to go?"

The mouse looked this way, then that way, this way, that way, this way. Then he pointed to his left. "This way!" he said.

"No," said the tortoise, "that way." He pointed to the right.

"No!" cried the mouse, "this way!" He pointed to the left.

The grandmother became confused. The tortoise was pointing one way, and the mouse was pointing another!

She did not know which way to go. The rain kept pouring and the sun was still nowhere to be seen.

She walked on and on. But the grandmother was unable to tell if she was walking "this way" or "that way".

Soon it became dark and the grandmother rested under a tree.

Suddenly she heard a sound in the tree: "Hoeee! Hoehoeee!"

It was an owl.

"What do you want, old woman?" asked the owl.

"Owl, can you please tell me which way to go?" she asked.

"Where do you want to go, old woman?" the owl wanted to know.

"To the end of the world!"

"Hoee! Hoee! Hoee!" said the owl. "Why do you want to go to the end of the world, old woman?"

"I want to see where the sun sleeps," she said.

"Hoee! Hoee! Hoee!" the owl laughed. "The sun cannot sleep!"

The old woman became angry with the owl. "Why do you say the sun cannot sleep, Owl?" she asked.

The owl blinked. This old woman was very silly! "Didn't you know the sun is very, very hot?" he asked her.

"Yes, I know the sun is very, very hot!" she said.

"Then the sun cannot stand still at one place, old woman," he said.

"Why not?"

"Because it will burn everything to death, old woman!"

The old woman stood for a while. Yes, it was true what the owl said. The sun could get very hot. But, the sun was not shining now, she thought: "Could it be that the sun was sleeping somewhere?"

The owl had no more to say about the sun and its mysterious ways.

So the grandmother decided to go on by herself and look for the end of the world.

She walked and she walked. For days she walked in the rain. The sun was nowhere to be seen. By now the old grandmother didn't know where she was.

Still, she walked.

One day the grandmother became too tired to walk. So she sat down and slept. She was so tired that she did not dream at all.

When she woke up the next morning, there was not a cloud in the sky. The sun had come out again!

The grandmother was glad to see the sun.

She sat in the sun until her clothes were dry. She sat and looked around her, and what did she see? She was back at her old home again!

The grandmother was very glad to be back. She unpacked and made herself some food and swept the yard.

But the following day she began to ask herself: "If the sun could stand still, where will it stand still? Will it stand still at the end of the world, or at the beginning of the world?"

The grandmother thought and thought. Then she decided to pack some clothes and food and set out to look for...

... the beginning of the world!

Something about the Author and Illustrator

DINAH M. MBANZE

taught at a farm school in the district of Bronkhorstspruit in Gauteng until 1998, when, after thirty years, she was retrenched because she lacked formal teaching qualifications. At the suggestion of Jo Bleeker of Tweefontein farm where Dinah lives, she then started to write down the tales she had heard as a child. With the assistence of Jo Bleeker the stories were later prepared and presented for publication.

NIKI DALY

is an international award-winning illustrator and writer of children's picture books. In 1995 *All the Magic in the World* earned him an IBBY Honours Award for Illustration, and the New York Times Literary Supplement selected his *Why the Sun and Moon Live in the Sky* as one of the ten best illustrated books published in the USA that year. In 1996 the same book won the Anne Izard Story Teller's Choice Award, and in 1998 *Bravo, Zan Angelo* received the Parent's Choice Award for Illustration. Niki lives in Cape Town in the Western Cape.